Plato

Menexenus; Eryxias

in large print

Plato

Menexenus; Eryxias

in large print

Reproduction of the original.

1st Edition 2022 | ISBN: 978-3-36831-191-9

Verlag (Publisher): Outlook Verlag GmbH, Zeilweg 44, 60439 Frankfurt, Deutschland
Vertretungsberechtigt (Authorized to represent): E. Roepke, Zeilweg 44, 60439 Frankfurt, Deutschland
Druck (Print): Books on Demand GmbH, In de Tarpen 42, 22848 Norderstedt, Deutschland

MENEXENUS

ERYXIAS

by Plato

Translated by Benjamin Jowett

MENEXENUS

APPENDIX I.

It seems impossible to separate by any exact line the genuine writings of Plato from the spurious. The only external evidence to them which is of much value is that of Aristotle; for the Alexandrian catalogues of a century later include manifest forgeries. Even the value of the Aristotelian authority is a good deal impaired by the uncertainty concerning the date and authorship of the writings which are ascribed to him. And several of the citations of Aristotle omit the name of Plato, and some of them omit the name of the dialogue from which they are taken. Prior, however, to the enquiry about the writings of a particular author, general considerations which equally affect all evidence to the genuineness of ancient writings are the following: Shorter works are more likely to have been forged, or to have received an erroneous designation, than longer ones; and some kinds of composition, such as epistles or panegyrical orations, are more liable to suspicion than others; those, again, which have a taste of sophistry in them, or the ring of a later age, or the slighter character of a rhetorical exercise, or in which a motive or some affinity to spurious writings can be detected, or which seem to have originated in a name or statement really occurring in some classical author, are

3

also of doubtful credit; while there is no instance of any ancient writing proved to be a forgery, which combines excellence with length. A really great and original writer would have no object in fathering his works on Plato; and to the forger or imitator, the 'literary hack' of Alexandria and Athens, the Gods did not grant originality or genius. Further, in attempting to balance the evidence for and against a Platonic dialogue, we must not forget that the form of the Platonic writing was common to several of his contemporaries. Aeschines, Euclid, Phaedo, Antisthenes, and in the next generation Aristotle, are all said to have composed dialogues; and mistakes of names are very likely to have occurred. Greek literature in the third century before Christ was almost as voluminous as our own, and without the safeguards of regular publication, or printing, or binding, or even of distinct titles. An unknown writing was naturally attributed to a known writer whose works bore the same character; and the name once appended easily obtained authority. A tendency may also be observed to blend the works and opinions of the master with those of his scholars. To a later Platonist, the difference between Plato and his imitators was not so perceptible as to ourselves. The Memorabilia of Xenophon and the Dialogues of Plato are but a part of a considerable Socratic literature which has passed away. And we must consider how we should regard the question of the genuineness of a particular writing, if this lost literature had been preserved to us.

These considerations lead us to adopt the following criteria of genuineness: (1) That is most certainly Plato's which Aristotle attributes to him by name, which (2) is of considerable length, of (3) great excellence, and also (4) in harmony with the general spirit of the Platonic writings. But the testimony of Aristotle cannot always be distinguished from that of a later age (see above); and has various degrees of importance. Those writings which he cites without mentioning Plato, under their own names, e.g. the Hippias, the Funeral Oration, the Phaedo, etc., have an inferior degree of evidence in their favour. They may have been supposed by him to be the writings of another, although in the case of really great works, e.g. the Phaedo, this is not credible; those again which are quoted but not named, are still more defective in their external credentials. There may be also a possibility that Aristotle was mistaken, or may have confused the master and his scholars in the case of a short writing; but this is inconceivable about a more important work, e.g. the Laws, especially when we remember that he was living at Athens, and a frequenter of the groves of the Academy, during the last twenty years of Plato's life. Nor must we forget that in all his numerous citations from the Platonic writings he never attributes any passage found in the extant dialogues to any one but Plato. And lastly, we may remark that one or two great writings, such as the Parmenides and the Politicus, which are wholly devoid of Aristotelian (1) credentials may be fairly attributed to Plato, on the ground of (2) length, (3) excellence, and (4) accordance with the general spirit of his writings. Indeed the greater part of the evidence for the genuineness of ancient Greek authors may be summed up under two heads only: (1)

excellence; and (2) uniformity of tradition—a kind of evidence, which though in many cases sufficient, is of inferior value.

Proceeding upon these principles we appear to arrive at the conclusion that nineteen-twentieths of all the writings which have ever been ascribed to Plato, are undoubtedly genuine. There is another portion of them, including the Epistles, the Epinomis, the dialogues rejected by the ancients themselves, namely, the Axiochus, De justo, De virtute, Demodocus, Sisyphus, Eryxias, which on grounds, both of internal and external evidence, we are able with equal certainty to reject. But there still remains a small portion of which we are unable to affirm either that they are genuine or spurious. They may have been written in youth, or possibly like the works of some painters, may be partly or wholly the compositions of pupils; or they may have been the writings of some contemporary transferred by accident to the more celebrated name of Plato, or of some Platonist in the next generation who aspired to imitate his master. Not that on grounds either of language or philosophy we should lightly reject them. Some difference of style, or inferiority of execution, or inconsistency of thought, can hardly be considered decisive of their spurious character. For who always does justice to himself, or who writes with equal care at all times? Certainly not Plato, who exhibits the greatest differences in dramatic power, in the formation of sentences, and in the use of words, if his earlier writings are compared with his later ones, say the Protagoras or Phaedrus with the Laws. Or who can be expected to think in the same manner

6

during a period of authorship extending over above fifty years, in an age of great intellectual activity, as well as of political and literary transition? Certainly not Plato, whose earlier writings are separated from his later ones by as wide an interval of philosophical speculation as that which separates his later writings from Aristotle.

The dialogues which have been translated in the first Appendix, and which appear to have the next claim to genuineness among the Platonic writings, are the Lesser Hippias, the Menexenus or Funeral Oration, the First Alcibiades. Of these, the Lesser Hippias and the Funeral Oration are cited by Aristotle; the first in the Metaphysics, the latter in the Rhetoric. Neither of them are expressly attributed to Plato, but in his citation of both of them he seems to be referring to passages in the extant dialogues. From the mention of 'Hippias' in the singular by Aristotle, we may perhaps infer that he was unacquainted with a second dialogue bearing the same name. Moreover, the mere existence of a Greater and Lesser Hippias, and of a First and Second Alcibiades, does to a certain extent throw a doubt upon both of them. Though a very clever and ingenious work, the Lesser Hippias does not appear to contain anything beyond the power of an imitator, who was also a careful student of the earlier Platonic writings, to invent. The motive or leading thought of the dialogue may be detected in Xen. Mem., and there is no similar instance of a 'motive' which is taken from Xenophon in an undoubted dialogue of Plato. On the other hand, the upholders of the genuineness of the dialogue will find in the Hippias a true Socratic spirit;

they will compare the Ion as being akin both in subject and treatment; they will urge the authority of Aristotle; and they will detect in the treatment of the Sophist, in the satirical reasoning upon Homer, in the reductio ad absurdum of the doctrine that vice is ignorance, traces of a Platonic authorship. In reference to the last point we are doubtful, as in some of the other dialogues, whether the author is asserting or overthrowing the paradox of Socrates, or merely following the argument 'whither the wind blows.' That no conclusion is arrived at is also in accordance with the character of the earlier dialogues. The resemblances or imitations of the Gorgias, Protagoras, and Euthydemus, which have been observed in the Hippias, cannot with certainty be adduced on either side of the argument. On the whole, more may be said in favour of the genuineness of the Hippias than against it.

The Menexenus or Funeral Oration is cited by Aristotle, and is interesting as supplying an example of the manner in which the orators praised 'the Athenians among the Athenians,' falsifying persons and dates, and casting a veil over the gloomier events of Athenian history. It exhibits an acquaintance with the funeral oration of Thucydides, and was, perhaps, intended to rival that great work. If genuine, the proper place of the Menexenus would be at the end of the Phaedrus. The satirical opening and the concluding words bear a great resemblance to the earlier dialogues; the oration itself is professedly a mimetic work, like the speeches in the Phaedrus, and cannot therefore be tested by a comparison of the other writings of Plato. The funeral oration of Pericles is expressly mentioned in the Phaedrus, and this may have suggested the subject, in the same manner that the Cleitophon appears to be suggested by the slight mention of Cleitophon and his attachment to Thrasymachus in the Republic; and the Theages by the mention of Theages in the Apology and Republic; or as the Second Alcibiades seems to be founded upon the text of Xenophon, Mem. A similar taste for parody appears not only in the Phaedrus, but in the Protagoras, in the Symposium, and to a certain extent in the Parmenides.

To these two doubtful writings of Plato I have added the First Alcibiades, which, of all the disputed dialogues of Plato, has the greatest merit, and is somewhat longer than any of them, though not verified by the testimony of Aristotle, and in many respects at variance with the Symposium in the description of the relations of Socrates and Alcibiades. Like the Lesser Hippias and the Menexenus, it is to be compared to the earlier writings of Plato. The motive of the piece may, perhaps, be found in that passage of the Symposium in which Alcibiades describes himself as self-convicted by the words of Socrates. For the disparaging manner in which Schleiermacher has spoken of this dialogue there seems to be no sufficient foundation. At the same time, the lesson imparted is simple, and the irony more transparent than in the undoubted dialogues of Plato. We know, too, that Alcibiades was a favourite thesis, and that at least five or six dialogues bearing this name passed current in antiquity, and are attributed to contemporaries of Socrates and Plato. (1) In the entire absence of real external evidence (for the catalogues of the Alexandrian librarians cannot be regarded as trustworthy); and (2) in the absence of the highest marks either of poetical or philosophical excellence; and (3) considering that we have express testimony to the existence of contemporary writings bearing the name of Alcibiades, we are compelled to suspend our judgment on the genuineness of the extant dialogue.

Neither at this point, nor at any other, do we propose to draw an absolute line of demarcation between genuine and spurious writings of Plato. They fade off imperceptibly from one class to another. There may have been degrees of genuineness in the dialogues themselves, as there are certainly degrees of evidence by which they are supported. The traditions of the oral discourses both of Socrates and Plato may have formed the basis of semi-Platonic writings; some of them may be of the same mixed character which is apparent in Aristotle and Hippocrates, although the form of them is different. But the writings of Plato, unlike the writings of Aristotle, seem never to have been confused with the writings of his disciples: this was probably due to their definite form, and to their inimitable excellence. The three dialogues which we have offered in the Appendix to the criticism of the reader may be partly spurious and partly genuine; they may be altogether spurious;—that is an alternative which must be frankly admitted. Nor can we maintain of some other dialogues, such as the Parmenides, and the Sophist, and Politicus, that no considerable objection can be urged against them, though greatly overbalanced by the weight (chiefly) of internal evidence in their favour. Nor,

10

on the other hand, can we exclude a bare possibility that some dialogues which are usually rejected, such as the Greater Hippias and the Cleitophon, may be genuine. The nature and object of these semi-Platonic writings require more careful study and more comparison of them with one another, and with forged writings in general, than they have yet received, before we can finally decide on their character. We do not consider them all as genuine until they can be proved to be spurious, as is often maintained and still more often implied in this and similar discussions; but should say of some of them, that their genuineness is neither proven nor disproven until further evidence about them can be adduced. And we are as confident that the Epistles are spurious, as that the Republic, the Timaeus, and the Laws are genuine.

On the whole, not a twentieth part of the writings which pass under the name of Plato, if we exclude the works rejected by the ancients themselves and two or three other plausible inventions, can be fairly doubted by those who are willing to allow that a considerable change and growth may have taken place in his philosophy (see above). That twentieth debatable portion scarcely in any degree affects our judgment of Plato, either as a thinker or a writer, and though suggesting some interesting questions to the scholar and critic, is of little importance to the general reader.

INTRODUCTION.

The Menexenus has more the character of a rhetorical exercise than any other of the Platonic works. The writer seems to have wished to emulate Thucydides, and the far slighter work of Lysias. In his rivalry with the latter, to whom in the Phaedrus Plato shows a strong antipathy, he is entirely successful, but he is not equal to Thucydides. The Menexenus, though not without real Hellenic interest, falls very far short of the rugged grandeur and political insight of the great historian. The fiction of the speech having been invented by Aspasia is well sustained, and is in the manner of Plato, notwithstanding the anachronism which puts into her mouth an allusion to the peace of Antalcidas, an event occurring forty years after the date of the supposed oration. But Plato, like Shakespeare, is careless of such anachronisms, which are not supposed to strike the mind of the reader. The effect produced by these grandiloquent orations on Socrates, who does not recover after having heard one of them for three days and more, is truly Platonic.

Such discourses, if we may form a judgment from the three which are extant (for the so-called Funeral Oration of Demosthenes is a bad and spurious imitation of Thucydides and Lysias), conformed to a regular type. They began with Gods and ancestors, and the legendary history of Athens, to which succeeded an almost equally fictitious account of later times. The Persian war usually formed the centre of the narrative; in the age of Isocrates and Demosthenes the Athenians were still living on the glories of Marathon and

Salamis. The Menexenus veils in panegyric the weak places of Athenian history. The war of Athens and Boeotia is a war of liberation; the Athenians gave back the Spartans taken at Sphacteria out of kindness—indeed, the only fault of the city was too great kindness to their enemies, who were more honoured than the friends of others (compare Thucyd., which seems to contain the germ of the idea); we democrats are the aristocracy of virtue, and the like. These are the platitudes and falsehoods in which history is disguised. The taking of Athens is hardly mentioned.

The author of the Menexenus, whether Plato or not, is evidently intending to ridicule the practice, and at the same time to show that he can beat the rhetoricians in their own line, as in the Phaedrus he may be supposed to offer an example of what Lysias might have said, and of how much better he might have written in his own style. The orators had recourse to their favourite loci communes, one of which, as we find in Lysias, was the shortness of the time allowed them for preparation. But Socrates points out that they had them always ready for delivery, and that there was no difficulty in improvising any number of such orations. To praise the Athenians among the Athenians was easy,—to praise them among the Lacedaemonians would have been a much more difficult task. Socrates himself has turned rhetorician, having learned of a woman, Aspasia, the mistress of Pericles; and any one whose teachers had been far inferior to his own—say, one who had learned from Antiphon the Rhamnusian—would be quite equal to the task of praising men to themselves. When we remember that

Antiphon is described by Thucydides as the best pleader of his day, the satire on him and on the whole tribe of rhetoricians is transparent.

The ironical assumption of Socrates, that he must be a good orator because he had learnt of Aspasia, is not coarse, as Schleiermacher supposes, but is rather to be regarded as fanciful. Nor can we say that the offer of Socrates to dance naked out of love for Menexenus, is any more un-Platonic than the threat of physical force which Phaedrus uses towards Socrates. Nor is there any real vulgarity in the fear which Socrates expresses that he will get a beating from his mistress, Aspasia: this is the natural exaggeration of what might be expected from an imperious woman. Socrates is not to be taken seriously in all that he says, and Plato, both in the Symposium and elsewhere, is not slow to admit a sort of Aristophanic humour. How a great original genius like Plato might or might not have written, what was his conception of humour, or what limits he would have prescribed to himself, if any, in drawing the picture of the Silenus Socrates, are problems which no critical instinct can determine.

On the other hand, the dialogue has several Platonic traits, whether original or imitated may be uncertain. Socrates, when he departs from his character of a 'know nothing' and delivers a speech, generally pretends that what he is speaking is not his own composition. Thus in the Cratylus he is run away with; in the Phaedrus he has heard somebody say something—is inspired by the genius loci; in the Symposium he derives his wisdom from Diotima of Mantinea, and the like. But he does not impose on

Menexenus by his dissimulation. Without violating the character of Socrates, Plato, who knows so well how to give a hint, or some one writing in his name, intimates clearly enough that the speech in the Menexenus like that in the Phaedrus is to be attributed to Socrates. The address of the dead to the living at the end of the oration may also be compared to the numerous addresses of the same kind which occur in Plato, in whom the dramatic element is always tending to prevail over the rhetorical. The remark has been often made, that in the Funeral Oration of Thucydides there is no allusion to the existence of the dead. But in the Menexenus a future state is clearly, although not strongly, asserted.

Whether the Menexenus is a genuine writing of Plato, or an imitation only, remains uncertain. In either case, the thoughts are partly borrowed from the Funeral Oration of Thucydides; and the fact that they are so, is not in favour of the genuineness of the work. Internal evidence seems to leave the question of authorship in doubt. There are merits and there are defects which might lead to either conclusion. The form of the greater part of the work makes the enquiry difficult; the introduction and the finale certainly wear the look either of Plato or of an extremely skilful imitator. The excellence of the forgery may be fairly adduced as an argument that it is not a forgery at all. In this uncertainty the express testimony of Aristotle, who quotes, in the Rhetoric, the well-known words, 'It is easy to praise the Athenians among the Athenians,' from the Funeral Oration, may perhaps turn the balance in its favour. It must be remembered also that the work was famous in antiquity, and is included in the Alexandrian catalogues of Platonic writings.

MENEXENUS

PERSONS OF THE DIALOGUE:
Socrates and Menexenus.

SOCRATES: Whence come you, Menexenus? Are you from the Agora?

MENEXENUS: Yes, Socrates; I have been at the Council.

SOCRATES: And what might you be doing at the Council? And yet I need hardly ask, for I see that you, believing yourself to have arrived at the end of education and of philosophy, and to have had enough of them, are mounting upwards to things higher still, and, though rather young for the post, are intending to govern us elder men, like the rest of your family, which has always provided some one who kindly took care of us.

MENEXENUS: Yes, Socrates, I shall be ready to hold office, if you allow and advise that I should, but not if you think otherwise. I went to the council chamber because I heard that the Council was about to choose some one who was to speak over the dead. For you know that there is to be a public funeral?

SOCRATES: Yes, I know. And whom did they choose?

16

MENEXENUS: No one; they delayed the election until tomorrow, but I believe that either Archinus or Dion will be chosen.

SOCRATES: O Menexenus! Death in battle is certainly in many respects a noble thing. The dead man gets a fine and costly funeral, although he may have been poor, and an elaborate speech is made over him by a wise man who has long ago prepared what he has to say, although he who is praised may not have been good for much. The speakers praise him for what he has done and for what he has not done—that is the beauty of them—and they steal away our souls with their embellished words; in every conceivable form they praise the city; and they praise those who died in war, and all our ancestors who went before us; and they praise ourselves also who are still alive, until I feel quite elevated by their laudations, and I stand listening to their words, Menexenus, and become enchanted by them, and all in a moment I imagine myself to have become a greater and nobler and finer man than I was before. And if, as often happens, there are any foreigners who accompany me to the speech, I become suddenly conscious of having a sort of triumph over them, and they seem to experience a corresponding feeling of admiration at me, and at the greatness of the city, which appears to them, when they are under the influence of the speaker, more wonderful than ever. This consciousness of dignity lasts me more than three days, and not until the fourth or fifth day do I come to my senses and know where I am; in the meantime I have been living in the Islands of the Blest. Such is the art of our

17

rhetoricians, and in such manner does the sound of their words keep ringing in my ears.

MENEXENUS: You are always making fun of the rhetoricians, Socrates; this time, however, I am inclined to think that the speaker who is chosen will not have much to say, for he has been called upon to speak at a moment's notice, and he will be compelled almost to improvise.

SOCRATES: But why, my friend, should he not have plenty to say? Every rhetorician has speeches ready made; nor is there any difficulty in improvising that sort of stuff. Had the orator to praise Athenians among Peloponnesians, or Peloponnesians among Athenians, he must be a good rhetorician who could succeed and gain credit. But there is no difficulty in a man's winning applause when he is contending for fame among the persons whom he is praising.

MENEXENUS: Do you think not, Socrates?

SOCRATES: Certainly 'not.'

MENEXENUS: Do you think that you could speak yourself if there should be a necessity, and if the Council were to choose you?

SOCRATES: That I should be able to speak is no great wonder, Menexenus, considering that I have an excellent mistress in the art of rhetoric,—she who has made so many good speakers, and one who was the best among all the Hellenes—Pericles, the son of Xanthippus.

MENEXENUS: And who is she? I suppose that you mean Aspasia.

18

SOCRATES: Yes, I do; and besides her I had Connus, the son of Metrobius, as a master, and he was my master in music, as she was in rhetoric. No wonder that a man who has received such an education should be a finished speaker; even the pupil of very inferior masters, say, for example, one who had learned music of Lamprus, and rhetoric of Antiphon the Rhamnusian, might make a figure if he were to praise the Athenians among the Athenians.

MENEXENUS: And what would you be able to say if you had to speak?

SOCRATES: Of my own wit, most likely nothing; but yesterday I heard Aspasia composing a funeral oration about these very dead. For she had been told, as you were saying, that the Athenians were going to choose a speaker, and she repeated to me the sort of speech which he should deliver, partly improvising and partly from previous thought, putting together fragments of the funeral oration which Pericles spoke, but which, as I believe, she composed.

MENEXENUS: And can you remember what Aspasia said?

SOCRATES: I ought to be able, for she taught me, and she was ready to strike me because I was always forgetting.

MENEXENUS: Then why will you not rehearse what she said?

SOCRATES: Because I am afraid that my mistress may be angry with me if I publish her speech.

MENEXENUS: Nay, Socrates, let us have the speech, whether Aspasia's or any one else's, no matter. I hope that you will oblige me.

19

SOCRATES: But I am afraid that you will laugh at me if I continue the games of youth in old age.

MENEXENUS: Far otherwise, Socrates; let us by all means have the speech.

SOCRATES: Truly I have such a disposition to oblige you, that if you bid me dance naked I should not like to refuse, since we are alone. Listen then: If I remember rightly, she began as follows, with the mention of the dead:—(Thucyd.)

There is a tribute of deeds and of words. The departed have already had the first, when going forth on their destined journey they were attended on their way by the state and by their friends; the tribute of words remains to be given to them, as is meet and by law ordained. For noble words are a memorial and a crown of noble actions, which are given to the doers of them by the hearers. A word is needed which will duly praise the dead and gently admonish the living, exhorting the brethren and descendants of the departed to imitate their virtue, and consoling their fathers and mothers and the survivors, if any, who may chance to be alive of the previous generation. What sort of a word will this be, and how shall we rightly begin the praises of these brave men? In their life they rejoiced their own friends with their valour, and their death they gave in exchange for the salvation of the living. And I think that we should praise them in the order in which nature made them good, for they were good because they were sprung from good fathers. Wherefore let us first of all praise the goodness of their birth; secondly, their nurture and education; and then let us set forth how noble their actions were, and how worthy of the education which they had received.

And first as to their birth. Their ancestors were not strangers, nor are these their descendants sojourners only, whose fathers have come from another country; but they are the children of the soil, dwelling and living in their own land. And the country which brought them up is not like other countries, a stepmother to her children, but their own true mother; she bore them and nourished them and received them, and in her bosom they now repose. It is meet and right, therefore, that we should begin by praising the land which is their mother, and that will be a way of praising their noble birth.

The country is worthy to be praised, not only by us, but by all mankind; first, and above all, as being dear to the Gods. This is proved by the strife and contention of the Gods respecting her. And ought not the country which the Gods praise to be praised by all mankind? The second praise which may be fairly claimed by her, is that at the time when the whole earth was sending forth and creating diverse animals, tame and wild, she our mother was free and pure from savage monsters, and out of all animals selected and brought forth man, who is superior to the rest in understanding, and alone has justice and religion. And a great proof that she brought forth the common ancestors of us and of the departed, is that she provided the means of support for her offspring. For as a woman proves her motherhood by giving milk to her young ones (and she who has no fountain of milk is not a mother), so did this our land prove that she was the mother of men, for in those days she alone and first of all brought forth wheat and barley for human food, which is the best and noblest sustenance for man, whom she regarded as her true offspring. And these are truer proofs of motherhood in a country than in a woman, for the woman in her conception and generation is but the imitation of the earth, and not the earth of the woman. And of the fruit of the earth she gave a plenteous supply, not only to her own, but to others also; and afterwards she made the olive to spring up to be a boon to her children, and to help them in their toils. And when she had herself nursed them and brought them up to manhood, she gave them Gods to be their rulers and teachers, whose names are well known, and need not now be repeated. They are the Gods who first ordered our lives, and instructed us in the arts for the supply of our daily needs, and taught us the acquisition and use of arms for the defence of the country.

Thus born into the world and thus educated, the ancestors of the departed lived and made themselves a government, which I ought briefly to commemorate. For government is the nurture of man, and the government of good men is good, and of bad men bad. And I must show that our ancestors were trained under a good government, and for this reason they were good, and our contemporaries are also good, among whom our departed friends are to be reckoned. Then as now, and indeed always, from that time to this, speaking generally, our government was an aristocracy—a form of government which receives various names, according to the fancies of men, and is sometimes called democracy, but is really an aristocracy or government of the best which has the approval of the many. For kings we have always had, first hereditary and then elected, and authority is mostly in the hands of the people, who dispense offices and power to those who appear to be most deserving of them. Neither is a man rejected from weakness or poverty or obscurity of origin, nor honoured by reason of the opposite, as in other states, but there is one principle—he who appears to be wise and good is a governor and ruler. The basis of this our government is equality of birth; for other states are made up of all sorts and unequal conditions of men, and therefore their governments are unequal; there are tyrannies and there are oligarchies, in which the one party are slaves and the others masters. But we and our citizens are brethren, the children all of one mother, and we do not think it right to be one another's masters or servants; but the natural equality of birth compels us to seek for legal equality, and to recognize no superiority except in the reputation of virtue and wisdom.

And so their and our fathers, and these, too, our brethren, being nobly born and having been brought up in all freedom, did both in their public and private capacity many noble deeds famous over the whole world. They were the deeds of men who thought that they ought to fight both against Hellenes for the sake of Hellenes on behalf of freedom, and against barbarians in the common interest of Hellas. Time would fail me to tell of their defence of their country against the invasion of Eumolpus and the Amazons, or of their defence of the Argives against the Cadmeians, or of the

Heracleids against the Argives; besides, the poets have already declared in song to all mankind their glory, and therefore any commemoration of their deeds in prose which we might attempt would hold a second place. They already have their reward, and I say no more of them; but there are other worthy deeds of which no poet has worthily sung, and which are still wooing the poet's muse. Of these I am bound to make honourable mention, and shall invoke others to sing of them also in lyric and other strains, in a manner becoming the actors. And first I will tell how the Persians, lords of Asia, were enslaving Europe, and how the children of this land, who were our fathers, held them back. Of these I will speak first, and praise their valour, as is meet and fitting. He who would rightly estimate them should place himself in thought at that time, when the whole of Asia was subject to the third king of Persia. The first king, Cyrus, by his valour freed the Persians, who were his countrymen, and subjected the Medes, who were their lords, and he ruled over the rest of Asia, as far as Egypt; and after him came his son, who ruled all the accessible part of Egypt and Libya; the third king was Darius, who extended the land boundaries of the empire to Scythia, and with his fleet held the sea and the islands. None presumed to be his equal; the minds of all men were enthralled by him—so many and mighty and warlike nations had the power of Persia subdued. Now Darius had a quarrel against us and the Eretrians, because, as he said, we had conspired against Sardis, and he sent 500,000 men in transports and vessels of war, and 300 ships, and Datis as commander, telling him to bring the Eretrians and Athenians to the king, if he wished to keep his head on his shoulders. He sailed against the Eretrians, who were reputed to be amongst the noblest and most warlike of the Hellenes of that day, and they were numerous, but he conquered them all in three days; and when he had conquered them, in order that no one might escape, he searched the whole country after this manner: his soldiers, coming to the borders of Eretria and spreading from sea to sea, joined hands and passed through the whole country, in order that they might be able to tell the king that no one had escaped them. And from Eretria they went to Marathon with a like intention, expecting to bind the Athenians in the same yoke of necessity in which they had bound the Eretrians. Having effected one-half of their purpose, they were in the act of attempting the other, and none of the Hellenes dared to assist either the Eretrians or the Athenians, except the Lacedaemonians, and they arrived a day too late for the battle; but the rest were panic-stricken and kept quiet, too happy in having escaped for a time. He who has present to his mind that conflict will know what manner of men they were who received the onset of the barbarians at Marathon, and chastened the pride of the whole of Asia, and by the victory which they gained over the barbarians first taught other men that the power of the Persians was not invincible, but that hosts of men and the multitude of riches alike yield to valour. And I assert that those men are the fathers not only of ourselves, but of our liberties and of the liberties of all who are on the continent, for that was the action to which the Hellenes looked back when they ventured to fight for their own safety in the battles which ensued: they became disciples of the men of Marathon. To them, therefore, I assign in my speech the first place, and the second to those who fought and conquered in the sea fights at Salamis and Artemisium; for of them, too, one might have many things to say—of the assaults which they endured by sea and land, and how they repelled them. I will mention only that act of theirs which appears to me to be the noblest, and which followed that of Marathon and came nearest to it; for the men of Marathon only showed the Hellenes that it was possible to ward off the barbarians by land, the many by the few; but there was no proof that they could be defeated by ships, and at sea the Persians retained the reputation of being invincible in numbers and wealth and skill and strength. This is the glory of the men who fought at sea, that they dispelled the second terror which had hitherto possessed the Hellenes, and so made the fear of numbers, whether of ships or men, to cease among them. And so the soldiers of Marathon and the sailors of Salamis became the schoolmasters of Hellas; the one teaching and habituating the Hellenes not to fear the barbarians at sea, and the others not to fear them by land. Third in order, for the number and valour of the combatants, and third in the salvation of Hellas, I place the battle of Plataea. And now the Lacedaemonians as well as the Athenians took part in the struggle; they were all united in this greatest and most terrible conflict of all; wherefore their virtues will be celebrated in times to come, as they are now celebrated by us. But at a later period many Hellenic tribes were still on the side of the barbarians, and there was a report that the great king was going to make a new attempt upon the Hellenes, and therefore justice requires that we should also make mention of those who crowned the previous work of our salvation, and drove and purged away all barbarians from the sea. These were the men who fought by sea at the river Eurymedon, and who went on the expedition to Cyprus, and who sailed to Egypt and divers other places; and they should be gratefully remembered by us, because they compelled the king in fear for himself to look to his own safety instead of plotting the destruction of Hellas.

And so the war against the barbarians was fought out to the end by the whole city on their own behalf, and on behalf of their countrymen. There was peace, and our city was held in honour; and then, as prosperity makes men jealous, there succeeded a jealousy of her, and jealousy begat envy, and so she became engaged against her will in a war with the Hellenes. On the breaking out of war, our citizens met the Lacedaemonians at Tanagra, and fought for the freedom of the Boeotians; the issue was doubtful, and was decided by the engagement which followed. For when the Lacedaemonians had gone on their way, leaving the Boeotians, whom they were aiding, on the third day after the battle of Tanagra, our countrymen conquered at Oenophyta, and righteously restored those who had been unrighteously exiled. And they were the first after the Persian war who fought on behalf of liberty in aid of Hellenes against Hellenes; they were brave men, and freed those whom they aided, and were the first too who were honourably interred in this sepulchre by the state. Afterwards there was a mighty war, in which all the Hellenes joined, and devastated our country, which was very ungrateful of them; and our countrymen, after defeating them in a naval engagement and taking their leaders, the Spartans, at Sphagia, when they might have destroyed them, spared their lives, and gave them back, and made peace, considering that they should war with the fellow-countrymen only until they gained a victory over them, and not because of the private anger of the state destroy the common interest of Hellas; but that with barbarians they should war to the death. Worthy of praise are they also who waged this war, and are here interred; for they proved, if any one doubted the superior prowess of the Athenians in the former war with the barbarians, that their doubts had no foundation—showing by their victory in the civil war with Hellas, in which they subdued the other chief state of the Hellenes, that they could conquer single-handed those with whom they had been allied in the war against the barbarians. After the peace there followed a third war, which was of a terrible and desperate nature, and in this many brave men who are here interred lost their lives—many of them had won victories in Sicily, whither they had gone over the seas to fight for the liberties of the Leontines, to whom they were bound by oaths; but, owing to the distance, the city was unable to help them, and they lost heart and came to misfortune, their very enemies and opponents winning more renown for valour and temperance than the friends of others. Many also fell in naval engagements at the Hellespont, after having in one day

28

taken all the ships of the enemy, and defeated them in other naval engagements. And what I call the terrible and desperate nature of the war, is that the other Hellenes, in their extreme animosity towards the city, should have entered into negotiations with their bitterest enemy, the king of Persia, whom they, together with us, had expelled;—him, without us, they again brought back, barbarian against Hellenes, and all the hosts, both of Hellenes and barbarians, were united against Athens. And then shone forth the power and valour of our city. Her enemies had supposed that she was exhausted by the war, and our ships were blockaded at Mitylene. But the citizens themselves embarked, and came to the rescue with sixty other ships, and their valour was confessed of all men, for they conquered their enemies and delivered their friends. And yet by some evil fortune they were left to perish at sea, and therefore are not interred here. Ever to be remembered and honoured are they, for by their valour not only that sea-fight was won for us, but the entire war was decided by them, and through them the city gained the reputation of being invincible, even though attacked by all mankind. And that reputation was a true one, for the defeat which came upon us was our own doing. We were never conquered by others, and to this day we are still unconquered by them; but we were our own conquerors, and received defeat at our own hands. Afterwards there was quiet and peace abroad, but there sprang up war at home; and, if men are destined to have civil war, no one could have desired that his city should take the disorder in a milder form. How joyful and natural was the reconciliation of those who came from the Piraeus and those who came from the city; with what moderation did they order the war against the tyrants in Eleusis, and in a manner how unlike what the other Hellenes expected! And the reason of this gentleness was the veritable tie of blood, which created among them a friendship as of kinsmen, faithful not in word only, but in deed. And we ought also to remember those who then fell by one another's hands, and on such occasions as these to reconcile them with sacrifices and prayers, praying to those who have power over them, that they may be reconciled even as we are reconciled. For they did not attack one another out of malice or enmity, but they were unfortunate. And that such was the fact we ourselves are witnesses, who are of the same race with them, and have mutually received and granted forgiveness of what we have done and suffered. After this there was perfect peace, and the city had rest; and her feeling was that she forgave the barbarians, who had severely suffered at her hands and severely retaliated, but that she was indignant at the ingratitude of the Hellenes, when she remembered how they had received good from her and returned evil, having made common cause with the barbarians, depriving her of the ships which had once been their salvation, and dismantling our walls, which had preserved their own from falling. She thought that she would no longer defend the Hellenes, when enslaved either by one another or by the barbarians, and did accordingly. This was our feeling, while the Lacedaemonians were thinking that we who were the champions of liberty had fallen, and that their business was to subject the remaining Hellenes. And why should I say more? for the events of which I am speaking happened not long ago and we can all of us remember how the chief peoples of Hellas, Argives and Boeotians and Corinthians, came to feel the need of us, and, what is the greatest miracle of all, the Persian king himself was driven to such extremity as to come round to the opinion, that from this city, of which he was the destroyer, and from no other, his salvation would proceed.

And if a person desired to bring a deserved accusation against our city, he would find only one charge which he could justly urge—that she was too compassionate and too favourable to the weaker side. And in this instance she was not able to hold out or keep her resolution of refusing aid to her injurers when they were being enslaved, but she was softened, and did in fact send out aid, and delivered the Hellenes from slavery, and they were free until they afterwards enslaved themselves. Whereas, to the great king she refused to give the assistance of the state, for she could not forget the trophies of Marathon and Salamis and Plataea; but she allowed exiles and volunteers to assist him, and they were his salvation. And she herself, when she was compelled, entered into the war, and built walls and ships, and fought with the Lacedaemonians on behalf of the Parians. Now the king fearing this city and wanting to stand aloof, when he saw the Lacedaemonians growing weary of the war at sea, asked of us, as the price of his alliance with us and the other allies, to give up the Hellenes in Asia, whom the Lacedaemonians had previously handed over to him, he thinking that we should refuse, and that then he might have

31

a pretence for withdrawing from us. About the other allies he was mistaken, for the Corinthians and Argives and Boeotians, and the other states, were quite willing to let them go, and swore and covenanted, that, if he would pay them money, they would make over to him the Hellenes of the continent, and we alone refused to give them up and swear. Such was the natural nobility of this city, so sound and healthy was the spirit of freedom among us, and the instinctive dislike of the barbarian, because we are pure Hellenes, having no admixture of barbarism in us. For we are not like many others, descendants of Pelops or Cadmus or Egyptus or Danaus, who are by nature barbarians, and yet pass for Hellenes, and dwell in the midst of us; but we are pure Hellenes, uncontaminated by any foreign element, and therefore the hatred of the foreigner has passed unadulterated into the life-blood of the city. And so, notwithstanding our noble sentiments, we were again isolated, because we were unwilling to be guilty of the base and unholy act of giving up Hellenes to barbarians. And we were in the same case as when we were subdued before; but, by the favour of Heaven, we managed better, for we ended the war without the loss of our ships or walls or colonies; the enemy was only too glad to be quit of us. Yet in this war we lost many brave men, such as were those who fell owing to the ruggedness of the ground at the battle of Corinth, or by treason at Lechaeum. Brave men, too, were those who delivered the Persian king, and drove the Lacedaemonians from the sea. I remind you of them, and you must celebrate them together with me, and do honour to their memories.

Such were the actions of the men who are here interred, and of others who have died on behalf of their country; many and glorious things I have spoken of them, and there are yet many more and more glorious things remaining to be told—many days and nights would not suffice to tell of them. Let them not be forgotten, and let every man remind their descendants that they also are soldiers who must not desert the ranks of their ancestors, or from cowardice fall behind. Even as I exhort you this day, and in all future time, whenever I meet with any of you, shall continue to remind and exhort you, O ye sons of heroes, that you strive to be the bravest of men. And I think that I ought now to repeat what your fathers desired to have said to you who are their survivors, when they went out to battle, in case anything happened to them. I will tell you what I heard them say, and what, if they had only speech, they would fain be saying, judging from what they then said. And you must imagine that you hear them saying what I now repeat to you:—

'Sons, the event proves that your fathers were brave men; for we might have lived dishonourably, but have preferred to die honourably rather than bring you and your children into disgrace, and rather than dishonour our own fathers and forefathers; considering that life is not life to one who is a dishonour to his race, and that to such a one neither men nor Gods are friendly, either while he is on the earth or after death in the world below. Remember our words, then, and whatever is your aim let virtue be the condition of the attainment of your aim, and know that without this all possessions and pursuits are dishonourable and evil. For

33

neither does wealth bring honour to the owner, if he be a coward; of such a one the wealth belongs to another, and not to himself. Nor does beauty and strength of body, when dwelling in a base and cowardly man, appear comely, but the reverse of comely, making the possessor more conspicuous, and manifesting forth his cowardice. And all knowledge, when separated from justice and virtue, is seen to be cunning and not wisdom; wherefore make this your first and last and constant and all-absorbing aim, to exceed, if possible, not only us but all your ancestors in virtue; and know that to excel you in virtue only brings us shame, but that to be excelled by you is a source of happiness to us. And we shall most likely be defeated, and you will most likely be victors in the contest, if you learn so to order your lives as not to abuse or waste the reputation of your ancestors, knowing that to a man who has any self-respect, nothing is more dishonourable than to be honoured, not for his own sake, but on account of the reputation of his ancestors. The honour of parents is a fair and noble treasure to their posterity, but to have the use of a treasure of wealth and honour, and to leave none to your successors, because you have neither money nor reputation of your own, is alike base and dishonourable. And if you follow our precepts you will be received by us as friends, when the hour of destiny brings you hither; but if you neglect our words and are disgraced in your lives, no one will welcome or receive you. This is the message which is to be delivered to our children.

'Some of us have fathers and mothers still living, and we would urge them, if, as is likely, we shall die, to bear the calamity as lightly as possible, and not to condole with one another; for they have sorrows enough, and will not need any one to stir them up. While we gently heal their wounds, let us remind them that the Gods have heard the chief part of their prayers; for they prayed, not that their children might live for ever, but that they might be brave and renowned. And this, which is the greatest good, they have attained. A mortal man cannot expect to have everything in his own life turning out according to his will; and they, if they bear their misfortunes bravely, will be truly deemed brave fathers of the brave. But if they give way to their sorrows, either they will be suspected of not being our parents, or we of not being such as our panegyrists declare. Let not either of the two alternatives happen, but rather let them be our chief and true panegyrists, who show in their lives that they are true men, and had men for their sons. Of old the saying, "Nothing too much," appeared to be, and really was, well said. For he whose happiness rests with himself, if possible, wholly, and if not, as far as is possible,—who is not hanging in suspense on other men, or changing with the vicissitude of their fortune,—has his life ordered for the best. He is the temperate and valiant and wise; and when his riches come and go, when his children are given and taken away, he will remember the proverb—"Neither rejoicing overmuch nor grieving overmuch," for he relies upon himself. And such we would have our parents to be—that is our word and wish, and as such we now offer ourselves, neither lamenting overmuch, nor fearing overmuch, if we are to die at this time. And we entreat our fathers and mothers to retain these feelings throughout their future life, and to be assured that they will not please us by sorrowing and lamenting over us. But, if the dead have any knowledge of the living, they will displease us most by making themselves miserable and by taking their misfortunes too much to heart, and they will please us best if they bear their loss lightly and temperately. For our life will have the noblest end which is vouchsafed to man, and should be glorified rather than lamented. And if they will direct their minds to the care and nurture of our wives and children, they will soonest forget their misfortunes, and live in a better and nobler way, and be dearer to us.

'This is all that we have to say to our families: and to the state we would say—Take care of our parents and of our sons: let her worthily cherish the old age of our parents, and bring up our sons in the right way. But we know that she will of her own accord take care of them, and does not need any exhortation of ours.'

This, O ye children and parents of the dead, is the message which they bid us deliver to you, and which I do deliver with the utmost seriousness. And in their name I beseech you, the children, to imitate your fathers, and you, parents, to be of good cheer about yourselves; for we will nourish your age, and take care of you both publicly and privately in any place in which one of us may meet one of you who are the parents of the dead. And the care of you which the city shows, you know yourselves; for she has made provision by law concerning the parents and children of those who die in war; the highest authority is specially entrusted with the duty of watching over them above all other citizens, and they will see that your fathers and mothers have no wrong done to them. The city herself shares in the education of the children, desiring as far as it is possible that their orphanhood may not be felt by them; while they are children she is a parent to them, and when they have arrived at man's estate she sends them to their several duties, in full armour clad; and bringing freshly to their minds the ways of their fathers, she places in their hands the instruments of their fathers' virtues; for the sake of the omen, she would have them from the first begin to rule over their own houses arrayed in the strength and arms of their fathers. And as for the dead, she never ceases honouring them, celebrating in common for all rites which become the property of each; and in addition to this, holding gymnastic and equestrian contests, and musical festivals of every sort. She is to the dead in the place of a son and heir, and to their sons in the place of a father, and to their parents and elder kindred in the place of a guardian—ever and always caring for them. Considering this, you ought to bear your calamity the more gently; for thus you will be most endeared to the dead and to the living, and your sorrows will heal and be healed. And now do you and all, having lamented the dead in common according to the law, go your ways.

You have heard, Menexenus, the oration of Aspasia the Milesian.

MENEXENUS: Truly, Socrates, I marvel that Aspasia, who is only a woman, should be able to compose such a speech; she must be a rare one.

SOCRATES: Well, if you are incredulous, you may come with me and hear her.

MENEXENUS: I have often met Aspasia, Socrates, and know what she is like.

SOCRATES: Well, and do you not admire her, and are you not grateful for her speech?

MENEXENUS: Yes, Socrates, I am very grateful to her or to him who told you, and still more to you who have told me.

SOCRATES: Very good. But you must take care not to tell of me, and then at some future time I will repeat to you many other excellent political speeches of hers.

MENEXENUS: Fear not, only let me hear them, and I will keep the secret.

SOCRATES: Then I will keep my promise.

ERYXIAS

APPENDIX II.

The two dialogues which are translated in the second appendix are not mentioned by Aristotle, or by any early authority, and have no claim to be ascribed to Plato. They are examples of Platonic dialogues to be assigned probably to the second or third generation after Plato, when his writings were well known at Athens and Alexandria. They exhibit considerable originality, and are remarkable for containing several thoughts of the sort which we suppose to be modern rather than ancient, and which therefore have a peculiar interest for us. The Second Alcibiades shows that the difficulties about prayer which have perplexed Christian theologians were not unknown among the followers of Plato. The Eryxias was doubted by the ancients themselves: yet it may claim the distinction of being, among all Greek or Roman writings, the one which anticipates in the most striking manner the modern science of political economy and gives an abstract form to some of its principal doctrines.

For the translation of these two dialogues I am indebted to my friend and secretary, Mr. Knight.

That the Dialogue which goes by the name of the Second Alcibiades is a genuine writing of Plato will not be maintained by any modern critic, and was hardly believed by the ancients themselves. The dialectic is poor and weak. There is no power over language, or beauty of style; and there is a certain abruptness and agroikia in the conversation, which is very un-Platonic. The best passage is probably that about the poets:—the remark that the poet, who is of a reserved disposition, is uncommonly difficult to understand, and the ridiculous interpretation of Homer, are entirely in the spirit of Plato (compare Protag; Ion; Apol.). The characters are ill-drawn. Socrates assumes the 'superior person' and preaches too much, while Alcibiades is stupid and heavy-in-hand. There are traces of Stoic influence in the general tone and phraseology of the Dialogue (compare opos melesei tis...kaka: oti pas aphron mainetai): and the writer seems to have been acquainted with the 'Laws' of Plato (compare Laws). An incident from the Symposium is rather clumsily introduced, and two somewhat hackneyed quotations (Symp., Gorg.) recur. The reference to the death of Archelaus as having occurred 'quite lately' is only a fiction, probably suggested by the Gorgias, where the story of Archelaus is told, and a similar phrase occurs;—ta gar echthes kai proen gegonota tauta, k.t.l. There are several passages which are either corrupt or extremely ill-expressed. But there is a modern interest in the subject of the dialogue; and it is a good example of a short spurious work, which may be attributed to the second or third century before Christ.

INTRODUCTION.

Much cannot be said in praise of the style or conception of the Eryxias. It is frequently obscure; like the exercise of a student, it is full of small imitations of Plato:—Phaeax returning from an expedition to Sicily (compare Socrates in the Charmides from the army at Potidaea), the figure of the game at draughts, borrowed from the Republic, etc. It has also in many passages the ring of sophistry. On the other hand, the rather unhandsome treatment which is exhibited towards Prodicus is quite unlike the urbanity of Plato.

Yet there are some points in the argument which are deserving of attention. (1) That wealth depends upon the need of it or demand for it, is the first anticipation in an abstract form of one of the great principles of modern political economy, and the nearest approach to it to be found in an ancient writer. (2) The resolution of wealth into its simplest implements going on to infinity is a subtle and refined thought. (3) That wealth is relative to circumstances is a sound conception. (4) That the arts and sciences which receive payment are likewise to be comprehended under the notion of wealth, also touches a question of modern political economy. (5) The distinction of post hoc and propter hoc, often lost sight of in modern as well as in ancient times. These metaphysical conceptions and distinctions show considerable power of thought in the writer, whatever we may think of his merits as an imitator of Plato.

ERYXIAS

PERSONS OF THE DIALOGUE:
Socrates, Eryxias, Erasistratus, Critias.

SCENE: The portico of a temple of Zeus.

It happened by chance that Eryxias the Steirian was walking with me in the Portico of Zeus the Deliverer, when there came up to us Critias and Erasistratus, the latter the son of Phaeax, who was the nephew of Erasistratus. Now Erasistratus had just arrived from Sicily and that part of the world. As they approached, he said, Hail, Socrates!

SOCRATES: The same to you, I said; have you any good news from Sicily to tell us?

ERASISTRATUS: Most excellent. But, if you please, let us first sit down; for I am tired with my yesterday's journey from Megara.

SOCRATES: Gladly, if that is your desire.

ERASISTRATUS: What would you wish to hear first? he said. What the Sicilians are doing, or how they are disposed towards our city? To my mind, they are very like wasps: so long as you only cause them a little annoyance they are quite unmanageable; you must destroy their nests if you wish to get the better of them. And in a similar way, the Syracusans, unless we set to work in earnest, and go against them with a great expedition, will never submit to our rule. The petty injuries which we at present inflict merely irritate them enough to make them utterly intractable. And now they have sent ambassadors to Athens, and intend, I suspect, to play us some trick.—While we were talking, the Syracusan envoys chanced to go by, and Erasistratus, pointing to one of them, said to me, That, Socrates, is the richest man in all Italy and Sicily. For who has larger estates or more land at his disposal to cultivate if he please? And they are of a quality, too, finer than any other land in Hellas. Moreover, he has all the things which go to make up wealth, slaves and horses innumerable, gold and silver without end.

I saw that he was inclined to expatiate on the riches of the man; so I asked him, Well, Erasistratus, and what sort of character does he bear in Sicily?

ERASISTRATUS: He is esteemed to be, and really is, the wickedest of all the Sicilians and Italians, and even more wicked than he is rich; indeed, if you were to ask any Sicilian whom he thought to be the worst and the richest of mankind, you would never hear any one else named.

I reflected that we were speaking, not of trivial matters, but about wealth and virtue, which are deemed to be of the greatest moment, and I asked Erasistratus whom he considered the wealthier,—he who was the possessor of a talent of silver or he who had a field worth two talents?

ERASISTRATUS: The owner of the field.

SOCRATES: And on the same principle he who had robes and bedding and such things which are of greater value to him than to a stranger would be richer than the stranger?

ERASISTRATUS: True.

SOCRATES: And if any one gave you a choice, which of these would you prefer?

ERASISTRATUS: That which was most valuable.

SOCRATES: In which way do you think you would be the richer?

ERASISTRATUS: By choosing as I said.

SOCRATES: And he appears to you to be the richest who has goods of the greatest value?

ERASISTRATUS: He does.

SOCRATES: And are not the healthy richer than the sick, since health is a possession more valuable than riches to the sick? Surely there is no one who would not prefer to be poor and well, rather than to have all the King of Persia's wealth and to be ill. And this proves that men set health above wealth, else they would never choose the one in preference to the other.

ERASISTRATUS: True.

SOCRATES: And if anything appeared to be more valuable than health, he would be the richest who possessed it?

ERASISTRATUS: He would.

SOCRATES: Suppose that some one came to us at this moment and were to ask, Well, Socrates and Eryxias and Erasistratus, can you tell me what is of the greatest value to men? Is it not that of which the possession will best enable a man to advise how his own and his friend's affairs should be administered?—What will be our reply?

ERASISTRATUS: I should say, Socrates, that happiness was the most precious of human possessions.

SOCRATES: Not a bad answer. But do we not deem those men who are most prosperous to be the happiest?

ERASISTRATUS: That is my opinion.

SOCRATES: And are they not most prosperous who commit the fewest errors in respect either of themselves or of other men?

ERASISTRATUS: Certainly.

SOCRATES: And they who know what is evil and what is good; what should be done and what should be left undone;—these behave the most wisely and make the fewest mistakes?

Erasistratus agreed to this.

SOCRATES: Then the wisest and those who do best and the most fortunate and the richest would appear to be all one and the same, if wisdom is really the most valuable of our possessions?

Yes, said Eryxias, interposing, but what use would it be if a man had the wisdom of Nestor and wanted the necessaries of life, food and drink and clothes and the like? Where would be the advantage of wisdom then? Or how could he be the richest of men who might even have to go begging, because he had not wherewithal to live?

I thought that what Eryxias was saying had some weight, and I replied, Would the wise man really suffer in this way, if he were so ill-provided; whereas if he had the house of Polytion, and the house were full of gold and silver, he would lack nothing?

ERYXIAS: Yes; for then he might dispose of his property and obtain in exchange what he needed, or he might sell it for money with which he could supply his wants and in a moment procure abundance of everything.

SOCRATES: True, if he could find some one who preferred such a house to the wisdom of Nestor. But if there are persons who set great store by wisdom like Nestor's and the advantages accruing from it, to sell these, if he were so disposed, would be easier still. Or is a house a most useful and necessary possession, and does it make a great difference in the comfort of life to have a mansion like Polytion's instead of living in a shabby little cottage, whereas wisdom is of small use and it is of no importance whether a man is wise or ignorant about the highest matters? Or is wisdom despised of men and can find no buyers, although cypress wood and marble of Pentelicus are eagerly bought by numerous purchasers? Surely the prudent pilot or the skilful physician, or the artist of any kind who is proficient in his art, is more worth than the things which are especially reckoned among riches; and he who can advise well and prudently for himself and others is able also to sell the product of his art, if he so desire.

Eryxias looked askance, as if he had received some unfair treatment, and said, I believe, Socrates, that if you were forced to speak the truth, you would declare that you were richer than Callias the son of Hipponicus. And yet, although you claimed to be wiser about things of real importance, you would not any the more be richer than he.

I dare say, Eryxias, I said, that you may regard these arguments of ours as a kind of game; you think that they have no relation to facts, but are like the pieces in the game

46

of draughts which the player can move in such a way that his opponents are unable to make any countermove. (Compare Republic.) And perhaps, too, as regards riches you are of opinion that while facts remain the same, there are arguments, no matter whether true or false, which enable the user of them to prove that the wisest and the richest are one and the same, although he is in the wrong and his opponents are in the right. There would be nothing strange in this; it would be as if two persons were to dispute about letters, one declaring that the word Socrates began with an S, the other that it began with an A, and the latter could gain the victory over the former.

Eryxias glanced at the audience, laughing and blushing at once, as if he had had nothing to do with what had just been said, and replied,—No, indeed, Socrates, I never supposed that our arguments should be of a kind which would never convince any one of those here present or be of advantage to them. For what man of sense could ever be persuaded that the wisest and the richest are the same? The truth is that we are discussing the subject of riches, and my notion is that we should argue respecting the honest and dishonest means of acquiring them, and, generally, whether they are a good thing or a bad.

Very good, I said, and I am obliged to you for the hint: in future we will be more careful. But why do not you yourself, as you introduced the argument, and do not think that the former discussion touched the point at issue, tell us whether you consider riches to be a good or an evil?

I am of opinion, he said, that they are a good. He was about to add something more, when Critias interrupted him:—Do you really suppose so, Eryxias?

Certainly, replied Eryxias; I should be mad if I did not: and I do not fancy that you would find any one else of a contrary opinion.

And I, retorted Critias, should say that there is no one whom I could not compel to admit that riches are bad for some men. But surely, if they were a good, they could not appear bad for any one?

Here I interposed and said to them: If you two were having an argument about equitation and what was the best way of riding, supposing that I knew the art myself, I should try to bring you to an agreement. For I should be ashamed if I were present and did not do what I could to prevent your difference. And I should do the same if you were quarrelling about any other art and were likely, unless you agreed on the point in dispute, to part as enemies instead of as friends. But now, when we are contending about a thing of which the usefulness continues during the whole of life, and it makes an enormous difference whether we are to regard it as beneficial or not,—a thing, too, which is esteemed of the highest importance by the Hellenes:—(for parents, as soon as their children are, as they think, come to years of discretion, urge them to consider how wealth may be acquired, since by riches the value of a man is judged):— When, I say, we are thus in earnest, and you, who agree in other respects, fall to disputing about a matter of such moment, that is, about wealth, and not merely whether it is

48

black or white, light or heavy, but whether it is a good or an evil, whereby, although you are now the dearest of friends and kinsmen, the most bitter hatred may arise betwixt you, I must hinder your dissension to the best of my power. If I could, I would tell you the truth, and so put an end to the dispute; but as I cannot do this, and each of you supposes that you can bring the other to an agreement, I am prepared, as far as my capacity admits, to help you in solving the question. Please, therefore, Critias, try to make us accept the doctrines which you yourself entertain.

CRITIAS: I should like to follow up the argument, and will ask Eryxias whether he thinks that there are just and unjust men?

ERYXIAS: Most decidedly.

CRITIAS: And does injustice seem to you an evil or a good?

ERYXIAS: An evil.

CRITIAS: Do you consider that he who bribes his neighbour's wife and commits adultery with her, acts justly or unjustly, and this although both the state and the laws forbid?

ERYXIAS: Unjustly.

CRITIAS: And if the wicked man has wealth and is willing to spend it, he will carry out his evil purposes? whereas he who is short of means cannot do what he fain would, and therefore does not sin? In such a case, surely, it is better that a person should not be wealthy, if his poverty prevents the accomplishment of his desires, and his desires are evil? Or, again, should you call sickness a good or an evil?

49

ERYXIAS: An evil.

CRITIAS: Well, and do you think that some men are intemperate?

ERYXIAS: Yes.

CRITIAS: Then, if it is better for his health that the intemperate man should refrain from meat and drink and other pleasant things, but he cannot owing to his intemperance, will it not also be better that he should be too poor to gratify his lust rather than that he should have a superabundance of means? For thus he will not be able to sin, although he desire never so much.

Critias appeared to be arguing so admirably that Eryxias, if he had not been ashamed of the bystanders, would probably have got up and struck him. For he thought that he had been robbed of a great possession when it became obvious to him that he had been wrong in his former opinion about wealth. I observed his vexation, and feared that they would proceed to abuse and quarrelling: so I said,—I heard that very argument used in the Lyceum yesterday by a wise man, Prodicus of Ceos; but the audience thought that he was talking mere nonsense, and no one could be persuaded that he was speaking the truth. And when at last a certain talkative young gentleman came in, and, taking his seat, began to laugh and jeer at Prodicus, tormenting him and demanding an explanation of his argument, he gained the ear of the audience far more than Prodicus.

Can you repeat the discourse to us? Said Erasistratus.

SOCRATES: If I can only remember it, I will. The youth began by asking Prodicus, In what way did he think that riches were a good and in what an evil? Prodicus answered, as you did just now, that they were a good to good men and to those who knew in what way they should be employed, while to the bad and the ignorant they were an evil. The same is true, he went on to say, of all other things; men make them to be what they are themselves. The saying of Archilochus is true:—

'Men's thoughts correspond to the things which they meet with.'

Well, then, replied the youth, if any one makes me wise in that wisdom whereby good men become wise, he must also make everything else good to me. Not that he concerns himself at all with these other things, but he has converted my ignorance into wisdom. If, for example, a person teach me grammar or music, he will at the same time teach me all that relates to grammar or music, and so when he makes me good, he makes things good to me.

Prodicus did not altogether agree: still he consented to what was said.

And do you think, said the youth, that doing good things is like building a house,—the work of human agency; or do things remain what they were at first, good or bad, for all time?

Prodicus began to suspect, I fancy, the direction which the argument was likely to take, and did not wish to be put down by a mere stripling before all those present:—(if they two had been alone, he would not have minded):—so he answered, cleverly enough: I think that doing good things is a work of human agency.

And is virtue in your opinion, Prodicus, innate or acquired by instruction?

The latter, said Prodicus.

Then you would consider him a simpleton who supposed that he could obtain by praying to the Gods the knowledge of grammar or music or any other art, which he must either learn from another or find out for himself?

Prodicus agreed to this also.

And when you pray to the Gods that you may do well and receive good, you mean by your prayer nothing else than that you desire to become good and wise:—if, at least, things are good to the good and wise and evil to the evil. But in that case, if virtue is acquired by instruction, it would appear that you only pray to be taught what you do not know.

Hereupon I said to Prodicus that it was no misfortune to him if he had been proved to be in error in supposing that the Gods immediately granted to us whatever we asked:—if, I added, whenever you go up to the Acropolis you earnestly entreat the Gods to grant you good things, although you know not whether they can yield your request, it is as though you went to the doors of the grammarian and begged him, although you had never made a study of the art, to give you a knowledge of grammar which would enable you forthwith to do the business of a grammarian.

While I was speaking, Prodicus was preparing to retaliate upon his youthful assailant, intending to employ the argument of which you have just made use; for he was annoyed to have it supposed that he offered a vain prayer to the Gods. But the master of the gymnasium came to him and begged him to leave because he was teaching the youths doctrines which were unsuited to them, and therefore bad for them.

I have told you this because I want you to understand how men are circumstanced in regard to philosophy. Had Prodicus been present and said what you have said, the audience would have thought him raving, and he would have been ejected from the gymnasium. But you have argued so excellently well that you have not only persuaded your hearers, but have brought your opponent to an agreement. For just as in the law courts, if two witnesses testify to the same fact, one of whom seems to be an honest fellow and the other a rogue, the testimony of the rogue often has the contrary effect on the judges' minds to what he intended, while the same evidence if given by the honest man at once strikes them as perfectly true. And probably the audience have something of the same feeling about yourself and Prodicus; they think him a Sophist and a braggart, and regard you as a gentleman of courtesy and worth. For they do not pay attention to the argument so much as to the character of the speaker.

But truly, Socrates, said Erasistratus, though you may be joking, Critias does seem to me to be saying something which is of weight.

SOCRATES: I am in profound earnest, I assure you. But why, as you have begun your argument so prettily, do you not go on with the rest? There is still something lacking, now you have agreed that (wealth) is a good to some and an evil to others. It remains to enquire what constitutes wealth; for unless you know this, you cannot possibly come to an understanding as to whether it is a good or an evil. I am ready to assist you in the enquiry to the utmost of my power: but first let him who affirms that riches are a good, tell us what, in his opinion, is wealth.

ERASISTRATUS: Indeed, Socrates, I have no notion about wealth beyond that which men commonly have. I suppose that wealth is a quantity of money (compare Arist. Pol.); and this, I imagine, would also be Critias' definition.

SOCRATES: Then now we have to consider, What is money? Or else later on we shall be found to differ about the question. For instance, the Carthaginians use money of this sort. Something which is about the size of a stater is tied up in a small piece of leather: what it is, no one knows but the makers. A seal is next set upon the leather, which then passes into circulation, and he who has the largest number of such pieces is esteemed the richest and best off. And yet if any one among us had a mass of such coins he would be no wealthier than if he had so many pebbles from the mountain. At Lacedaemon, again, they use iron by weight which has been rendered useless: and he who has the greatest mass of such iron is thought to be the richest, although elsewhere it has no value. In Ethiopia engraved stones are employed, of which a Lacedaemonian could make no use. Once more, among the Nomad Scythians a man who owned the house of Polytion would not be thought richer than one who possessed Mount Lycabettus among ourselves. And clearly those things cannot all be regarded as possessions; for in some cases the possessors would appear none the richer

54

thereby: but, as I was saying, some one of them is thought in one place to be money, and the possessors of it are the wealthy, whereas in some other place it is not money, and the ownership of it does not confer wealth; just as the standard of morals varies, and what is honourable to some men is dishonourable to others. And if we wish to enquire why a house is valuable to us but not to the Scythians, or why the Carthaginians value leather which is worthless to us, or the Lacedaemonians find wealth in iron and we do not, can we not get an answer in some such way as this: Would an Athenian, who had a thousand talents weight of the stones which lie about in the Agora and which we do not employ for any purpose, be thought to be any the richer?

ERASISTRATUS: He certainly would not appear so to me.

SOCRATES: But if he possessed a thousand talents weight of some precious stone, we should say that he was very rich?

ERASISTRATUS: Of course.

SOCRATES: The reason is that the one is useless and the other useful?

ERASISTRATUS: Yes.

SOCRATES: And in the same way among the Scythians a house has no value because they have no use for a house, nor would a Scythian set so much store on the finest house in the world as on a leather coat, because he could use the one and not the other. Or again, the Carthaginian coinage is not wealth in our eyes, for we could not employ it, as we can silver, to procure what we need, and therefore it is of no use to us.

ERASISTRATUS: True.

SOCRATES: What is useful to us, then, is wealth, and what is useless to us is not wealth?

But how do you mean, Socrates? said Eryxias, interrupting. Do we not employ in our intercourse with one another speech and violence (?) and various other things? These are useful and yet they are not wealth.

SOCRATES: Clearly we have not yet answered the question, What is wealth? That wealth must be useful, to be wealth at all,—thus much is acknowledged by every one. But what particular thing is wealth, if not all things? Let us pursue the argument in another way; and then we may perhaps find what we are seeking. What is the use of wealth, and for what purpose has the possession of riches been invented,—in the sense, I mean, in which drugs have been discovered for the cure of disease? Perhaps in this way we may throw some light on the question. It appears to be clear that whatever constitutes wealth must be useful, and that wealth is one class of useful things; and now we have to enquire, What is the use of those useful things which constitute wealth? For all things probably may be said to be useful which we use in production, just as all things which have life are animals, but there is a special kind of animal which we call 'man.' Now if any one were to ask us, What is that of which, if we were rid, we should not want medicine and the instruments of medicine, we might reply that this would be the case if disease were absent from our bodies and either never came to them at all or went away again as soon as it appeared; and we may therefore conclude that medicine is the science which is useful for getting rid of disease. But if we are further asked, What is that from which, if we were free, we should have no need of wealth? can we give an answer? If we have none, suppose that we restate the question thus:—If a man could live without food or drink, and yet suffer neither hunger nor thirst, would he want either money or anything else in order to supply his needs?

ERYXIAS: He would not.

SOCRATES: And does not this apply in other cases? If we did not want for the service of the body the things of which we now stand in need, and heat and cold and the other bodily sensations were unperceived by us, there would be no use in this so-called wealth, if no one, that is, had any necessity for those things which now make us wish for wealth in order that we may satisfy the desires and needs of the body in respect of our various wants. And therefore if the possession of wealth is useful in ministering to our bodily wants, and bodily wants were unknown to us, we should not need wealth, and possibly there would be no such thing as wealth.

ERYXIAS: Clearly not.

SOCRATES: Then our conclusion is, as would appear, that wealth is what is useful to this end?

Eryxias once more gave his assent, but the small argument considerably troubled him.

SOCRATES: And what is your opinion about another question:—Would you say that the same thing can be at one time useful and at another useless for the production of the same result?

ERYXIAS: I cannot say more than that if we require the same thing to produce the same result, then it seems to me to be useful; if not, not.

SOCRATES: Then if without the aid of fire we could make a brazen statue, we should not want fire for that purpose; and if we did not want it, it would be useless to us? And the argument applies equally in other cases.

ERYXIAS: Clearly.

SOCRATES: And therefore conditions which are not required for the existence of a thing are not useful for the production of it?

ERYXIAS: Of course not.

SOCRATES: And if without gold or silver or anything else which we do not use directly for the body in the way that we do food and drink and bedding and houses,—if without these we could satisfy the wants of the body, they would be of no use to us for that purpose?

ERYXIAS: They would not.

SOCRATES: They would no longer be regarded as wealth, because they are useless, whereas that would be wealth which enabled us to obtain what was useful to us?

ERYXIAS: O Socrates, you will never be able to persuade me that gold and silver and similar things are not wealth. But I am very strongly of opinion that things which are useless to us are not wealth, and that the money which is useful for this purpose is of the greatest use; not that these things are not useful towards life, if by them we can procure wealth.

SOCRATES: And how would you answer another question? There are persons, are there not, who teach music and grammar and other arts for pay, and thus procure those things of which they stand in need?

ERYXIAS: There are.

SOCRATES: And these men by the arts which they profess, and in exchange for them, obtain the necessities of life just as we do by means of gold and silver?

ERYXIAS: True.

SOCRATES: Then if they procure by this means what they want for the purposes of life, that art will be useful towards life? For do we not say that silver is useful because it enables us to supply our bodily needs?

ERYXIAS: We do.

SOCRATES: Then if these arts are reckoned among things useful, the arts are wealth for the same reason as gold and silver are, for, clearly, the possession of them gives wealth. Yet a little while ago we found it difficult to accept the argument which proved that the wisest are the wealthiest. But now there seems no escape from this conclusion. Suppose that we are asked, 'Is a horse useful to everybody?' will not our reply be, 'No, but only to those who know how to use a horse?'

ERYXIAS: Certainly.

SOCRATES: And so, too, physic is not useful to every one, but only to him who knows how to use it?

ERYXIAS: True.

SOCRATES: And the same is the case with everything else?

ERYXIAS: Yes.

SOCRATES: Then gold and silver and all the other elements which are supposed to make up wealth are only useful to the person who knows how to use them?

ERYXIAS: Exactly.

SOCRATES: And were we not saying before that it was the business of a good man and a gentleman to know where and how anything should be used?

ERYXIAS: Yes.

SOCRATES: The good and gentle, therefore will alone have profit from these things, supposing at least that they know how to use them. But if so, to them only will they seem to be wealth. It appears, however, that where a person is ignorant of riding, and has horses which are useless to him, if some one teaches him that art, he makes him also richer, for what was before useless has now become useful to him, and in giving him knowledge he has also conferred riches upon him.

ERYXIAS: That is the case.

SOCRATES: Yet I dare be sworn that Critias will not be moved a whit by the argument.

CRITIAS: No, by heaven, I should be a madman if I were. But why do you not finish the argument which proves that gold and silver and other things which seem to be wealth are not real wealth? For I have been exceedingly delighted to hear the discourses which you have just been holding.

SOCRATES: My argument, Critias (I said), appears to have given you the same kind of pleasure which you might have derived from some rhapsode's recitation of Homer; for you do not believe a word of what has been said. But come now, give me an answer to this question. Are not certain things useful to the builder when he is building a house?

CRITIAS: They are.

SOCRATES: And would you say that those things are useful which are employed in house building,—stones and bricks and beams and the like, and also the instruments with which the builder built the house, the beams and stones which they provided, and again the instruments by which these were obtained?

CRITIAS: It seems to me that they are all useful for building.

SOCRATES: And is it not true of every art, that not only the materials but the instruments by which we procure them and without which the work could not go on, are useful for that art?

CRITIAS: Certainly.

SOCRATES: And further, the instruments by which the instruments are procured, and so on, going back from stage to stage ad infinitum,—are not all these, in your opinion, necessary in order to carry out the work?

CRITIAS: We may fairly suppose such to be the case.

SOCRATES: And if a man has food and drink and clothes and the other things which are useful to the body, would he need gold or silver or any other means by which he could procure that which he now has?

CRITIAS: I do not think so.

SOCRATES: Then you consider that a man never wants any of these things for the use of the body?

CRITIAS: Certainly not.

SOCRATES: And if they appear useless to this end, ought they not always to appear useless? For we have already laid down the principle that things cannot be at one time useful and at another time not, in the same process.

CRITIAS: But in that respect your argument and mine are the same. For you maintain if they are useful to a certain end, they can never become useless; whereas I say that in order to accomplish some results bad things are needed, and good for others.

SOCRATES: But can a bad thing be used to carry out a good purpose?

CRITIAS: I should say not.

SOCRATES: And we call those actions good which a man does for the sake of virtue?

CRITIAS: Yes.

SOCRATES: But can a man learn any kind of knowledge which is imparted by word of mouth if he is wholly deprived of the sense of hearing?

CRITIAS: Certainly not, I think.

SOCRATES: And will not hearing be useful for virtue, if virtue is taught by hearing and we use the sense of hearing in giving instruction?

CRITIAS: Yes.

SOCRATES: And since medicine frees the sick man from his disease, that art too may sometimes appear useful in the acquisition of virtue, e.g. when hearing is procured by the aid of medicine.

CRITIAS: Very likely.

SOCRATES: But if, again, we obtain by wealth the aid of medicine, shall we not regard wealth as useful for virtue?

CRITIAS: True.

SOCRATES: And also the instruments by which wealth is procured?

CRITIAS: Certainly.

SOCRATES: Then you think that a man may gain wealth by bad and disgraceful means, and, having obtained the aid of medicine which enables him to acquire the power of hearing, may use that very faculty for the acquisition of virtue?

CRITIAS: Yes, I do.

SOCRATES: But can that which is evil be useful for virtue?

CRITIAS: No.

SOCRATES: It is not therefore necessary that the means by which we obtain what is useful for a certain object should always be useful for the same object: for it seems that bad actions may sometimes serve good purposes? The matter will be still plainer if we look at it in this way:—If things are useful towards the several ends for which they exist, which ends would not come into existence without them, how would you regard them? Can ignorance, for instance, be useful for knowledge, or disease for health, or vice for virtue?

CRITIAS: Never.

SOCRATES: And yet we have already agreed—have we not?—that there can be no knowledge where there has not previously been ignorance, nor health where there has not been disease, nor virtue where there has not been vice?

CRITIAS: I think that we have.

SOCRATES: But then it would seem that the antecedents without which a thing cannot exist are not necessarily useful to it. Otherwise ignorance would appear useful for knowledge, disease for health, and vice for virtue.

Critias still showed great reluctance to accept any argument which went to prove that all these things were useless. I saw that it was as difficult to persuade him as (according to the proverb) it is to boil a stone, so I said: Let us bid 'good-bye' to the discussion, since we cannot agree whether these things are useful and a part of wealth or not. But what shall we say to another question: Which is the happier and better man,—he who requires the greatest quantity of necessaries for body and diet, or he who requires only the fewest and least? The answer will perhaps become more obvious if we suppose some one, comparing the man himself at different times, to consider whether his condition is better when he is sick or when he is well?

CRITIAS: That is not a question which needs much consideration.

SOCRATES: Probably, I said, every one can understand that health is a better condition than disease. But when have we the greatest and the most various needs, when we are sick or when we are well?

CRITIAS: When we are sick.

SOCRATES: And when we are in the worst state we have the greatest and most especial need and desire of bodily pleasures?

CRITIAS: True.

SOCRATES: And seeing that a man is best off when he is least in need of such things, does not the same reasoning apply to the case of any two persons, of whom one has many and great wants and desires, and the other few and moderate? For instance, some men are gamblers, some drunkards, and some gluttons: and gambling and the love of drink and greediness are all desires?

CRITIAS: Certainly.

SOCRATES: But desires are only the lack of something: and those who have the greatest desires are in a worse condition than those who have none or very slight ones?

CRITIAS: Certainly I consider that those who have such wants are bad, and that the greater their wants the worse they are.

SOCRATES: And do we think it possible that a thing should be useful for a purpose unless we have need of it for that purpose?

CRITIAS: No.

SOCRATES: Then if these things are useful for supplying the needs of the body, we must want them for that purpose?

CRITIAS: That is my opinion.

SOCRATES: And he to whom the greatest number of things are useful for his purpose, will also want the greatest number of means of accomplishing it, supposing that we necessarily feel the want of all useful things?

CRITIAS: It seems so.

SOCRATES: The argument proves then that he who has great riches has likewise need of many things for the supply of the wants of the body; for wealth appears useful towards that end. And the richest must be in the worst condition, since they seem to be most in want of such things.

CONTENTS

Lightning Source UK Ltd.
Milton Keynes UK
UKHW010102100223
416720UK00001B/161